THE TALE OF
JEMIMA PUDDLE-DUCK
AND OTHER FARMYARD TALES

Four favourite Beatrix Potter stories which tell of farmyard comings and goings, mishaps and excitements, are all here in one special volume: *The Tale of Jemima Puddle-Duck, The Tale of Mr. Jeremy Fisher, The Tale of Mrs. Tiggy-Winkle* and *The Tale of Pigling Bland* all appear in full, accompanied by their original illustrations in this special large-format edition.

Beatrix Potter was born on 28 July 1866. She spent a lonely but interesting childhood and was encouraged to study art and natural history. She kept animals in her schoolroom – the original Peter Rabbit and Benjamin Bunny among them. She was educated by governesses, and it was for the little son of the last governess that the celebrated Peter Rabbit story was written – as a picture letter in 1893. She later had it turned into a book, first in a privately printed edition, then in 1902 with coloured pictures as the first of the series of little *Tales* which have become so popular throughout the world. Beatrix Potter died in 1943.

THE TALE OF
JEMIMA PUDDLE-DUCK
AND OTHER FARMYARD TALES

THE TALE OF MR. JEREMY FISHER · THE TALE OF MRS. TIGGY-WINKLE
THE TALE OF PIGLING BLAND

BY
BEATRIX POTTER ™
THE ORIGINAL AND AUTHORIZED EDITION

New colour reproductions

PUFFIN BOOKS

CONTENTS

THE TALE OF
JEMIMA PUDDLE-DUCK

A Farmyard Tale
for
Ralph and Betsy

WHAT a funny sight it is to see a brood of ducklings with a hen!

—Listen to the story of Jemima Puddle-duck, who was annoyed because the farmer's wife would not let her hatch her own eggs.

Her sister-in-law, Mrs. Rebeccah Puddle-duck, was perfectly willing to leave the hatching to some one else— 'I have not the patience to sit on a nest for twenty-eight days; and no more have you, Jemima. You would let them go cold; you know you would!'

'I wish to hatch my own eggs; I will hatch them all by myself,' quacked Jemima Puddle-duck.

She tried to hide her eggs; but they were always found and carried off.

Jemima Puddle-duck became quite desperate. She determined to make a nest right away from the farm.

She set off on a fine spring afternoon along the cart-road
that leads over the hill.

She was wearing a shawl and a poke bonnet.

When she reached the top of the hill, she saw a wood in
the distance.

She thought that it looked a safe quiet spot.

Jemima Puddle-duck was not much in the habit of flying. She ran downhill a few yards flapping her shawl, and then she jumped off into the air.

She flew beautifully when she had got a good start.

She skimmed along over the tree-tops until she saw an open place in the middle of the wood, where the trees and brushwood had been cleared.

Jemima alighted rather heavily, and began to waddle about in search of a convenient dry nesting-place. She rather fancied a tree-stump amongst some tall fox-gloves.

But—seated upon the stump, she was startled to find an elegantly dressed gentleman reading a newspaper.

He had black prick ears and sandy coloured whiskers.

'Quack?' said Jemima Puddle-duck, with her head and her bonnet on one side—'Quack?'

The gentleman raised his eyes above his newspaper and looked curiously at Jemima—

'Madam, have you lost your way?' said he. He had a long bushy tail which he was sitting upon, as the stump was somewhat damp.

Jemima thought him mighty civil and handsome. She explained that she had not lost her way, but that she was trying to find a convenient dry nesting-place.

'Ah! is that so? indeed!' said the gentleman with sandy whiskers, looking curiously at Jemima. He folded up the newspaper, and put it in his coat-tail pocket.

Jemima complained of the superfluous hen.

'Indeed! how interesting! I wish I could meet with that fowl. I would teach it to mind its own business!

'But as to a nest—there is no difficulty: I have a sackful of feathers in my wood-shed. No, my dear madam, you will be in nobody's way. You may sit there as long as you like,' said the bushy long-tailed gentleman.

He led the way to a very retired, dismal-looking house amongst the fox-gloves.

It was built of faggots and turf, and there were two broken pails, one on top of another, by way of a chimney.

'This is my summer residence; you would not find my earth—my winter house—so convenient,' said the hospitable gentleman.

There was a tumble-down shed at the back of the house, made of old soap-boxes. The gentleman opened the door, and showed Jemima in.

The shed was almost quite full of feathers—it was almost suffocating; but it was comfortable and very soft.

Jemima Puddle-duck was rather surprised to find such a vast quantity of feathers. But it was very comfortable; and she made a nest without any trouble at all.

When she came out, the sandy whiskered gentleman was sitting on a log reading the newspaper—at least he had it spread out, but he was looking over the top of it.

He was so polite, that he seemed almost sorry to let Jemima go home for the night. He promised to take great care of her nest until she came back again next day.

He said he loved eggs and ducklings; he should be proud to see a fine nestful in his wood-shed.

Jemima Puddle-duck came every afternoon; she laid nine eggs in the nest. They were greeny white and very large. The foxy gentleman admired them immensely. He used to turn them over and count them when Jemima was not there.

At last Jemima told him that she intended to begin to sit next day—'and I will bring a bag of corn with me, so that I need never leave my nest until the eggs are hatched. They might catch cold,' said the conscientious Jemima.

'Madam, I beg you not to trouble yourself with a bag; I will provide oats. But before you commence your tedious sitting, I intend to give you a treat. Let us have a dinner-party all to ourselves!

'May I ask you to bring up some herbs from the farm-garden to make a savoury omelette? Sage and thyme, and mint and two onions, and some parsley. I will provide lard for the stuff—lard for the omelette,' said the hospitable gentleman with sandy whiskers.

Jemima Puddle-duck was a simpleton: not even the mention of sage and onions made her suspicious.

She went round the farm-garden, nibbling off snippets of all the different sorts of herbs that are used for stuffing roast duck.

And she waddled into the kitchen, and got two onions out of a basket.

The collie-dog Kep met her coming out, 'What are you doing with those onions? Where do you go every afternoon by yourself, Jemima Puddle-duck?'

Jemima was rather in awe of the collie; she told him the whole story.

The collie listened, with his wise head on one side; he grinned when she described the polite gentleman with sandy whiskers.

He asked several questions about the wood, and about the exact position of the house and shed.

Then he went out, and trotted down the village. He went to look for two fox-hound puppies who were out at walk with the butcher.

Jemima Puddle-duck went up the cart-road for the last time, on a sunny afternoon. She was rather burdened with bunches of herbs and two onions in a bag.

She flew over the wood, and alighted opposite the house of the bushy long-tailed gentleman.

He was sitting on a log; he sniffed the air, and kept glancing uneasily round the wood. When Jemima alighted he quite jumped.

'Come into the house as soon as you have looked at your eggs. Give me the herbs for the omelette. Be sharp!'

He was rather abrupt. Jemima Puddle-duck had never heard him speak like that.

She felt surprised, and uncomfortable.

While she was inside she heard pattering feet round the back of the shed. Some one with a black nose sniffed at the bottom of the door, and then locked it.

Jemima became much alarmed.

A moment afterwards there were most awful noises—barking, baying, growls and howls, squealing and groans.

And nothing more was ever seen of that foxy-whiskered gentleman.

Presently Kep opened the door of the shed, and let out Jemima Puddle-duck.

Unfortunately the puppies rushed in and gobbled up all the eggs before he could stop them.

He had a bite on his ear and both the puppies were limping.

Jemima Puddle-duck was escorted home in tears on account of those eggs.

She laid some more in June, and she was permitted to keep them herself: but only four of them hatched.

Jemima Puddle-duck said that it was because of her nerves; but she had always been a bad sitter.

THE TALE OF
MR. JEREMY FISHER

*For
Stephanie
from
Cousin B.*

ONCE upon a time there was a frog called Mr. Jeremy Fisher; he lived in a little damp house amongst the buttercups at the edge of a pond.

The water was all slippy-sloppy in the larder and in the back passage.

But Mr. Jeremy liked getting his feet wet; nobody ever scolded him, and he never caught a cold!

He was quite pleased when he looked out and saw large drops of rain, splashing in the pond—

'I will get some worms and go fishing and catch a dish of minnows for my dinner,' said Mr. Jeremy Fisher. 'If I catch more than five fish, I will invite my friends Mr. Alderman Ptolemy Tortoise and Sir Isaac Newton. The Alderman, however, eats salad.'

Mr. Jeremy put on a macintosh, and a pair of shiny goloshes; he took his rod and basket, and set off with enormous hops to the place where he kept his boat.

The boat was round and green, and very like the other lily-leaves. It was tied to a water-plant in the middle of the pond.

Mr. Jeremy took a reed pole, and pushed the boat out into open water. 'I know a good place for minnows,' said Mr. Jeremy Fisher.

Mr. Jeremy stuck his pole into the mud and fastened his boat to it.

Then he settled himself cross-legged and arranged his fishing tackle. He had the dearest little red float. His rod was a tough stalk of grass, his line was a fine long white horse-hair, and he tied a little wriggling worm at the end.

The rain trickled down his back, and for nearly an hour he stared at the float.

'This is getting tiresome, I think I should like some lunch,' said Mr. Jeremy Fisher.

He punted back again amongst the water-plants, and took some lunch out of his basket.

'I will eat a butterfly sandwich, and wait till the shower is over,' said Mr. Jeremy Fisher.

A great big water-beetle came up underneath the lily leaf and tweaked the toe of one of his goloshes.

Mr. Jeremy crossed his legs up shorter, out of reach, and went on eating his sandwich.

Once or twice something moved about with a rustle and a splash amongst the rushes at the side of the pond.

'I trust that is not a rat,' said Mr. Jeremy Fisher; 'I think I had better get away from here.'

Mr. Jeremy shoved the boat out again a little way, and dropped in the bait. There was a bite almost directly; the float gave a tremendous bobbit!

'A minnow! a minnow! I have him by the nose!' cried Mr. Jeremy Fisher, jerking up his rod.

But what a horrible surprise! Instead of a smooth fat minnow, Mr. Jeremy landed little Jack Sharp the stickleback, covered with spines!

The stickleback floundered about the boat, pricking and snapping until he was quite out of breath. Then he jumped back into the water.

And a shoal of other little fishes put their heads out, and laughed at Mr. Jeremy Fisher.

And while Mr. Jeremy sat disconsolately on the edge of his boat—sucking his sore fingers and peering down into the water—a *much* worse thing happened; a really *frightful* thing it would have been, if Mr. Jeremy had not been wearing a macintosh!

A great big enormous trout came up—ker-pflop-p-p-p! with a splash—and it seized Mr. Jeremy with a snap, 'Ow! Ow! Ow!'—and then it turned and dived down to the bottom of the pond!

But the trout was so displeased with the taste of the macintosh, that in less than half a minute it spat him out again; and the only thing it swallowed was Mr. Jeremy's goloshes.

Mr. Jeremy bounced up to the surface of the water, like a cork and the bubbles out of a soda water bottle; and he swam with all his might to the edge of the pond.

He scrambled out on the first bank he came to, and he hopped home across the meadow with his macintosh all in tatters.

'What a mercy that was not a pike!' said Mr. Jeremy Fisher. 'I have lost my rod and basket; but it does not much matter, for I am sure I should never have dared to go fishing again!'

He put some sticking plaster on his fingers, and his friends both came to dinner. He could not offer them fish, but he had something else in his larder.

Sir Isaac Newton wore his black and gold waistcoat.

And Mr. Alderman Ptolemy Tortoise brought a salad with him in a string bag.

And instead of a nice dish of minnows—they had a roasted grasshopper with lady-bird sauce; which frogs consider a beautiful treat; but *I* think it must have been nasty!

THE TALE OF
MRS. TIGGY-WINKLE

for
The Real Little Lucie
of Newlands

ONCE upon a time there was a little girl called Lucie, who lived at a farm called Little-town. She was a good little girl—only she was always losing her pocket-handkerchiefs!

One day little Lucie came into the farm-yard crying—oh, she did cry so! 'I've lost my pocket-handkin! Three handkins and a pinny! Have *you* seen them, Tabby Kitten?'

The Kitten went on washing her white paws; so Lucie asked a speckled hen—

'Sally Henny-penny, have *you* found three pocket-handkins?'

But the speckled hen ran into a barn, clucking—

'I go barefoot, barefoot, barefoot!'

And then Lucie asked Cock Robin sitting on a twig. Cock Robin looked sideways at Lucie with his bright black eye, and he flew over a stile and away.

Lucie climbed upon the stile and looked up at the hill behind Little-town—a hill that goes up—up—into the clouds as though it had no top!

And a great way up the hill-side she thought she saw some white things spread upon the grass.

Lucie scrambled up the hill as fast as her stout legs would carry her; she ran along a steep path-way—up and up—until Little-town was right away down below—she could have dropped a pebble down the chimney!

Presently she came to a spring, bubbling out from the hill-side.

Some one had stood a tin can upon a stone to catch the water—but the water was already running over, for the can was no bigger than an egg-cup! And where the sand upon the path was wet—there were foot-marks of a *very* small person.

Lucie ran on, and on.

41

The path ended under a big rock. The grass was short and green, and there were clothes-props cut from bracken stems, with lines of plaited rushes, and a heap of tiny clothes pins—but no pocket-handkerchiefs!

But there was something else—a door! straight into the hill; and inside it some one was singing—

'Lily-white and clean, oh!
With little frills between, oh!
  Smooth and hot—red rusty
    spot
Never here be seen, oh!'

Lucie, knocked—once—twice, and interrupted the song. A little frightened voice called out 'Who's that?'

Lucie opened the door: and what do you think there was inside the hill?— a nice clean kitchen with a flagged floor and wooden beams—just like any other farm kitchen. Only the ceiling was so low that Lucie's head nearly touched it; and the pots and pans were small, and so was every-thing there.

There was a nice hot singey smell; and at the table, with an iron in her hand stood a very stout short person staring anxiously at Lucie.

Her print gown was tucked up, and she was wearing a large apron over her striped petticoat. Her little black nose went sniffle, sniffle, snuffle, and her eyes went twinkle, twinkle; and underneath her cap—where Lucie had yellow curls—that little person had PRICKLES!

'Who are you?' said Lucie. 'Have you seen my pocket-handkins?'

The little person made a bob-curtsey—'Oh, yes, if you please'm; my name is Mrs. Tiggy-winkle; oh, yes if you please'm, I'm an excellent clear-starcher!' And she took something out of a clothes-basket, and spread it on the ironing-blanket.

43

'What's that thing?' said Lucie—'that's not my pocket-handkin?'

'Oh no, if you please'm; that's a little scarlet waist-coat belonging to Cock Robin!'

And she ironed it and folded it, and put it on one side.

Then she took something else off a clothes-horse—

'That isn't my pinny?' said Lucie.

'Oh no, if you please'm; that's a damask table-cloth belonging to Jenny Wren; look how it's stained with currant wine! It's very bad to wash!' said Mrs. Tiggy-winkle.

Mrs. Tiggy-winkle's nose went sniffle, sniffle, snuffle, and her eyes went twinkle, twinkle; and she fetched another hot iron from the fire.

'There's one of my pocket-handkins!' cried Lucie—'and there's my pinny!'

Mrs. Tiggy-winkle ironed it, and goffered it, and shook out the frills.

'Oh that *is* lovely!' said Lucie.

'And what are those long yellow things with fingers like gloves?'

'Oh, that's a pair of stockings belonging to Sally Henny-penny—look how she's worn the heels out with scratching in the yard! She'll very soon go barefoot!' said Mrs. Tiggy-winkle.

'Why, there's another handkersniff—but it isn't mine; it's red?'

'Oh no, if you please'm; that one belongs to old Mrs. Rabbit; and it *did* so smell of onions! I've had to wash it separately, I can't get out the smell.'

'There's another one of mine,' said Lucie.

'What are those funny little white things?'

'That's a pair of mittens belonging to Tabby Kitten; I only have to iron them; she washes them herself.'

'There's my last pocket-handkin!' said Lucie.

'And what are you dipping into the basin of starch?'

'They're little dicky shirt-fronts belonging to Tom Titmouse—most terrible particular!' said Mrs. Tiggy-winkle. 'Now I've finished my ironing; I'm going to air some clothes.'

'What are these dear soft fluffy things?' said Lucie.

'Oh those are woolly coats belonging to the little lambs at Skelghyl.'

'Will their jackets take off?' asked Lucie.

'Oh yes, if you please'm; look at the sheep-mark on the shoulder. And here's one marked for Gatesgarth, and three that come from Little-town. They're *always* marked at washing!' said Mrs. Tiggy-winkle.

And she hung up all sorts and sizes of clothes—small brown coats of mice; and one velvety black mole-skin waist-coat; and a red tail-coat with no tail belonging to Squirrel Nutkin; and a very much shrunk blue jacket belonging to Peter Rabbit; and a petticoat, not marked, that had gone lost in the washing—and at last the basket was empty!

Then Mrs. Tiggy-winkle made tea—a cup for herself and a cup for Lucie. They sat before the fire on a bench and looked sideways at one another. Mrs. Tiggy-winkle's hand, holding the tea-cup, was very very brown, and very very wrinkly with the soap-suds; and all through her gown and her cap, there were *hair-pins* sticking wrong end out; so that Lucie didn't like to sit too near her.

When they had finished tea, they tied up the clothes in bundles; and Lucie's pocket-handkerchiefs were folded up inside her clean pinny, and fastened with a silver safety-pin.

And then they made up the fire with turf, and came out and locked the door, and hid the key under the door-sill.

Then away down the hill trotted Lucie and Mrs. Tiggy-winkle with the bundles of clothes!

All the way down the path little animals came out of the fern to meet them; the very first that they met were Peter Rabbit and Benjamin Bunny!

And she gave them their nice clean clothes; and all the little animals and birds were so very much obliged to dear Mrs. Tiggy-winkle.

So that at the bottom of the hill when they came to the stile, there was nothing left to carry except Lucie's one little bundle.

Lucie scrambled up the stile with the bundle in her hand; and then she turned to say 'Good-night,' and to thank the washer-woman— But what a *very* odd thing! Mrs. Tiggy-winkle had not waited either for thanks or for the washing bill!

She was running running running up the hill—and where was her white frilled cap? and her shawl? and her gown—and her petti-coat?

And *how* small she had grown—and *how* brown—and covered with Prickles!

Why! Mrs. Tiggy-winkle was nothing but a Hedgehog.

*   *   *   *   *

(Now some people say that little Lucie had been asleep upon the stile—but then how could she have found three clean pocket-handkins and a pinny, pinned with a silver safety-pin?

And besides—*I* have seen that door into the back of the hill called Cat Bells—and besides *I* am very well acquainted with dear Mrs. Tiggy-winkle!)

THE TALE OF
PIGLING BLAND

For
Cecily and Charlie

A Tale of
The Christmas Pig

ONCE upon a time there was an old pig called Aunt Pettitoes. She had eight of a family: four little girl pigs, called Cross-patch, Suck-suck, Yock-yock and Spot; and four little boy pigs, called Alexander, Pigling Bland, Chin-chin and Stumpy. Stumpy had had an accident to his tail.

The eight little pigs had very fine appetites. 'Yus, yus, yus! they eat and indeed they *do* eat!' said Aunt Pettitoes, looking at her family with pride. Suddenly there were fearful squeals; Alexander had squeezed inside the hoops of the pig trough and stuck.

Aunt Pettitoes and I dragged him out by the hind legs.

'Tchut, tut, tut! whichever is this?' grunted Aunt Pettitoes. Now all the pig family are pink, or pink with black spots, but this pig child was smutty black all over; when it had been popped into a tub, it proved to be Yock-yock.

Chin-chin was already in disgrace; it was washing day, and he had eaten a piece of soap. And presently in a basket of clean clothes, we found another dirty little pig.

I went into the garden; there I found Cross-patch and Suck-suck rooting up carrots. I whipped them myself and led them out by the ears. Cross-patch tried to bite me.

56

'Aunt Pettitoes, Aunt Pettitoes! you are a worthy person, but your family is not well brought up. Every one of them has been in mischief except Spot and Pigling Bland.'

'Yus, yus!' sighed Aunt Pettitoes. 'And they drink bucketfuls of milk; I shall have to get another cow! Good little Spot shall stay at home to do the housework; but the others must go. Four little boy pigs and four little girl pigs are too many altogether.' 'Yus, yus, yus,' said Aunt Pettitoes, 'there will be more to eat without them.'

So Chin-chin and Suck-suck went away in a wheel-barrow, and Stumpy, Yock-yock and Cross-patch rode away in a cart.

And the other two little boy pigs, Pigling Bland and Alexander, went to market. We brushed their coats, we curled their tails and washed their little faces, and wished them good-bye in the yard.

Aunt Pettitoes wiped her eyes with a large pocket handkerchief, then she wiped Pigling Bland's nose and shed tears; then she wiped Alexander's nose and shed tears; then she passed the handkerchief to Spot. Aunt Pettitoes sighed and grunted, and addressed those little pigs as follows:

'Now Pigling Bland, son Pigling Bland, you must go to market. Take your brother Alexander by the hand. Mind your Sunday clothes, and remember to blow your nose'— (Aunt Pettitoes passed round the handkerchief again)— 'beware of traps, hen roosts, bacon and eggs; always walk upon your hind legs.' Pigling Bland, who was a sedate little pig, looked solemnly at his mother, a tear trickled down his cheek.

Aunt Pettitoes turned to the other—'Now son Alexander take the hand '—'Wee, wee, wee!' giggled Alexander—'take the hand of your brother Pigling Bland, you must go to market. Mind—' 'Wee, wee, wee!' interrupted Alexander again. 'You put me out,' said Aunt Pettitoes—'Observe signposts and milestones; do not gobble herring bones—' 'And remember,' said I impressively, 'if you once cross the county boundary you cannot come back. Alexander, you are not attending. Here are two licences permitting two pigs to go to market in Lancashire. Attend, Alexander. I have had no end of trouble in getting these papers from the policeman.' Pigling Bland listened gravely; Alexander was hopelessly volatile.

I pinned the papers, for safety, inside their waistcoat pockets; Aunt Pettitoes gave to each a little bundle, and eight conversation peppermints with appropriate moral sentiments in screws of paper. Then they started.

Pigling Bland and Alexander trotted along steadily for a mile; at least Pigling Bland did. Alexander made the road half as long again by skipping from side to side. He danced about and pinched his brother, singing—

'This pig went to market, this pig stayed at home,
'This pig had a bit of meat—

let's see what they have given *us* for dinner, Pigling?'

Pigling Bland and Alexander sat down and untied their bundles. Alexander gobbled up his dinner in no time; he had already eaten all his own peppermints. 'Give me one of yours, please, Pigling.' 'But I wish to preserve them for emergencies,' said Pigling Bland doubtfully. Alexander went into squeals of laughter. Then he pricked Pigling with the pin that had fastened his pig paper; and when Pigling slapped him he dropped the pin, and tried to take Pigling's pin, and the papers got mixed up. Pigling Bland reproved Alexander.

But presently they made it up again, and trotted away together, singing—

'Tom, Tom, the piper's son, stole a pig
   and away he ran!
'But all the tune that he could play,
   was "Over the hills and far away!"'

'What's that, young sirs? Stole a pig? Where are your licences?' said the policeman. They had nearly run against him round a corner. Pigling Bland pulled out his paper; Alexander, after fumbling, handed over something scrumply—

'To 2½ oz. conversation sweeties at three farthings'—'What's this? This ain't a licence.' Alexander's nose lengthened visibly, he had lost it. 'I had one, indeed I had, Mr. Policeman!'

'It's not likely they let you start without. I am passing the farm. You may walk with me.' 'Can I come back too?'

inquired Pigling Bland. 'I see no reason, young sir; your paper is all right.' Pigling Bland did not like going on alone, and it was beginning to rain. But it is unwise to argue with the police; he gave his brother a peppermint, and watched him out of sight.

To conclude the adventures of Alexander—the policeman sauntered up to the house about tea time, followed by a damp subdued little pig. I disposed of Alexander in the neighbourhood; he did fairly well when he had settled down.

Pigling Bland went on alone dejectedly; he came to cross-roads and a sign-post—'To Market Town, 5 miles,' 'Over the Hills, 4 miles,' 'To Pettitoes Farm, 3 miles.'

Pigling Bland was shocked, there was little hope of sleeping in Market Town, and to-morrow was the hiring fair; it was deplorable to think how much time had been wasted by the frivolity of Alexander.

He glanced wistfully along the road towards the hills, and then set off walking obediently the other way, buttoning up his coat against the rain. He had never wanted to go; and the idea of standing all by himself in a crowded market, to be stared at, pushed, and hired by some big strange farmer was very disagreeable—

'I wish I could have a little garden and grow potatoes,' said Pigling Bland.

He put his cold hand in his pocket and felt his paper, he put his other hand in his other pocket and felt another paper—Alexander's! Pigling squealed; then ran back frantically, hoping to overtake Alexander and the policeman.

He took a wrong turn—several wrong turns, and was quite lost.

It grew dark, the wind whistled, the trees creaked and groaned.

Pigling Bland became frightened and cried 'Wee, wee, wee! I can't find my way home!'

After an hour's wandering he got out of the wood; the moon shone through the clouds, and Pigling Bland saw a country that was new to him.

The road crossed a moor; below was a wide valley with a river twinkling in the moonlight, and beyond, in misty distance, lay the hills.

He saw a small wooden hut, made his way to it, and crept inside—'I am afraid it *is* a hen house, but what can I do?' said Pigling Bland, wet and cold and quite tired out.

'Bacon and eggs, bacon and eggs!' clucked a hen on a perch.

'Trap, trap, trap! cackle, cackle, cackle!' scolded the disturbed cockerel. 'To market, to market! jiggetty jig!' clucked a broody white hen roosting next to him. Pigling Bland, much alarmed, determined to leave at daybreak. In the meantime, he and the hens fell asleep.

In less than an hour they were all awakened. The owner, Mr. Peter Thomas Piperson, came with a lantern and a hamper to catch six fowls to take to market in the morning.

He grabbed the white hen roosting next to the cock; then his eye fell upon Pigling Bland, squeezed up in a corner. He made a singular remark—'Hallo, here's another!'—seized Pigling by the scruff of the neck, and dropped him into the hamper. Then he dropped in five more dirty, kicking, cackling hens upon the top of Pigling Bland.

The hamper containing six fowls and a young pig was no light weight; it was taken down hill, unsteadily, with jerks. Pigling, although nearly scratched to pieces, contrived to hide the papers and peppermints inside his clothes.

At last the hamper was bumped down upon a kitchen floor, the lid was opened, and Pigling was lifted out. He looked up, blinking, and saw an offensively ugly elderly man, grinning from ear to ear.

'This one's come of himself, whatever,' said Mr. Piperson, turning Pigling's pockets inside out. He pushed the hamper into a corner, threw a sack over it to keep the hens quiet, put a pot on the fire, and unlaced his boots.

Pigling Bland drew forward a coppy stool, and sat on the edge of it, shyly warming his hands. Mr. Piperson pulled off a boot and threw it against the wainscot at the further end of the kitchen. There was a smothered noise—'Shut up!' said Mr. Piperson. Pigling Bland warmed his hands, and eyed him.

65

Mr. Piperson pulled off the other boot and flung it after the first, there was again a curious noise—'Be quiet, will ye?' said Mr. Piperson. Pigling Bland sat on the very edge of the coppy stool.

Mr. Piperson fetched meal from a chest and made porridge. It seemed to Pigling that something at the further end of the kitchen was taking a suppressed interest in the cooking, but he was too hungry to be troubled by noises.

Mr. Piperson poured out three platefuls: for himself, for Pigling, and a third—after glaring at Pigling—he put away with much scuffling, and locked up. Pigling Bland ate his supper discreetly.

After supper Mr. Piperson consulted an almanac, and felt Pigling's ribs; it was too late in the season for curing bacon, and he grudged his meal. Besides, the hens had seen this pig.

He looked at the small remains of a flitch, and then looked undecidedly at Pigling. 'You may sleep on the rug,' said Mr. Peter Thomas Piperson.

Pigling Bland slept like a top. In the morning Mr. Piperson made more porridge; the weather was warmer. He looked to see how much meal was left in the chest, and seemed dissatisfied—'You'll likely be moving on again?' said he to Pigling Bland.

Before Pigling could reply, a neighbour, who was giving Mr. Piperson and the hens a lift, whistled from the gate. Mr. Piperson hurried out with the hamper, enjoining Pigling to shut the door behind him and not meddle with nought; or 'I'll come back and skin ye!' said Mr. Piperson.

It crossed Pigling's mind that if *he* had asked for a lift, too, he might still have been in time for market.

But he distrusted Peter Thomas.

After finishing breakfast at his leisure, Pigling had a look round the cottage; everything was locked up. He found some potato peelings in a bucket in the back kitchen. Pigling ate the peel, and washed up the porridge plates in the bucket. He sang while he worked—

'Tom with his pipe made such a noise,
　He called up all the girls and boys—
'And they all ran to hear him play
　'"Over the hills and far away!"'

Suddenly a little smothered voice chimed in—

'Over the hills and a great way off,
　The wind shall blow my top knot off!'

Pigling Bland put down a plate which he was wiping, and listened.

After a long pause, Pigling went on tip-toe and peeped round the door into the front kitchen. There was nobody there.

After a long pause, Pigling went on tip-toe and peeped round the door into the front kitchen. There was nobody there.

After another pause, Pigling approached the door of the locked cupboard, and snuffed at the keyhole. It was quite quiet.

After another long pause, Pigling pushed a peppermint under the door. It was sucked in immediately.

In the course of the day Pigling pushed in all the remaining six peppermints.

When Mr. Piperson returned, he found Pigling sitting before the fire; he had brushed up the hearth and put on the pot to boil; the meal was not get-at-able.

Mr. Piperson was very affable; he slapped Pigling on the back, made lots of porridge and forgot to lock the meal chest. He did lock the cupboard door; but without properly shutting it. He went to bed early, and told Pigling upon no account to disturb him next day before twelve o'clock.

Pigling Bland sat by the fire, eating his supper.

All at once at his elbow, a little voice spoke—'My name is Pig-wig. Make me more porridge, please!' Pigling Bland jumped, and looked round.

A perfectly lovely little black Berkshire pig stood smiling beside him. She had twinkly little screwed up eyes, a double chin, and a short turned up nose.

She pointed at Pigling's plate; he hastily gave it to her, and fled to the meal chest. 'How did you come here?' asked Pigling Bland.

'Stolen,' replied Pig-wig, with her mouth full. Pigling helped himself to meal without scruple. 'What for?' 'Bacon, hams,' replied Pig-wig cheerfully. 'Why on earth don't you run away?' exclaimed the horrified Pigling.

'I shall after supper,' said Pig-wig decidedly.
Pigling Bland made more porridge and watched her shyly.

She finished a second plate, got up, and looked about her, as though she were going to start.

'You can't go in the dark,' said Pigling Bland.

Pig-wig looked anxious.

'Do you know your way by daylight?'

'I know we can see this little white house from the hills across the river. Which way are *you* going, Mr. Pig?'

'To market—I have two pig papers. I might take you to the bridge; if you have no objection,' said Pigling much confused and sitting on the edge of his coppy stool. Pig-wig's gratitude was such and she asked so many questions that it became embarrassing to Pigling Bland.

He was obliged to shut his eyes and pretend to sleep. She became quiet, and there was a smell of peppermint.

'I thought you had eaten them,' said Pigling, waking suddenly.

'Only the corners,' replied Pig-wig, studying the sentiments with much interest by the firelight.

'I wish you wouldn't; he might smell them through the ceiling,' said the alarmed Pigling.

Pig-wig put back the sticky peppermints into her pocket; 'Sing something,' she demanded.

'I am sorry ... I have toothache,' said Pigling much dismayed. 'Then I will sing,' replied Pig-wig. 'You will not mind if I say iddy tidditty? I have forgotten some of the words.'

Pigling Bland made no objection; he sat with his eyes half shut, and watched her.

She wagged her head and rocked about, clapping time and singing in a sweet little grunty voice—

> 'A funny old mother pig lived
> in a stye, and three little pig-
> gies had she;
> '(Ti idditty idditty) umph, umph,
> umph! and the little pigs said,
> wee, wee!'

She sang successfully through three or four verses, only at every verse her head nodded a little lower, and her little twinkly eyes closed up.

> 'Those three little piggies grew peaky and lean, and lean they might very
> well be;
> 'For somehow they couldn't say umph, umph, umph! and they wouldn't
> say wee, wee, wee!
> 'For somehow they couldn't say—

Pig-wig's head bobbed lower and lower, until she rolled over, a little round ball, fast asleep on the hearth-rug.

Pigling Bland, on tip-toe, covered her up with an anti-macassar.

He was afraid to go to sleep himself; for the rest of the night he sat listening to the chirping of the crickets and to the snores of Mr. Piperson overhead.

Early in the morning, between dark and daylight, Pigling tied up his little bundle and woke up Pigwig. She was excited and half-frightened.

'But it's dark! How can we find our way?'

'The cock has crowed; we must start before the hens come out; they might shout to Mr. Piperson.'

Pig-wig sat down again, and commenced to cry.

'Come away Pig-wig; we can see when we get used to it. Come! I can hear them clucking!'

Pigling had never said shuh! to a hen in his life, being peaceable; also he remembered the hamper.

He opened the house door quietly and shut it after them. There was no garden; the neighbourhood of Mr. Piperson's was all scratched up by fowls. They slipped away hand in hand across an untidy field to the road.

The sun rose while they were crossing the moor, a dazzle of light over the tops of the hills. The sunshine crept down the slopes into the peaceful green valleys, where little white cottages nestled in gardens and orchards.

'That's Westmorland,' said Pig-wig. She dropped Pigling's hand and commenced to dance, singing—

> 'Tom, Tom, the piper's son, stole a pig
>   and away he ran!
> 'But all the tune that he could play,
>   was "Over the hills and far away!"'

'Come, Pig-wig, we must get to the bridge before folks are stirring.' 'Why do you want to go to market, Pigling?' inquired Pig-wig presently. 'I don't want; I want to grow potatoes.' 'Have a peppermint?' said Pig-wig. Pigling Bland refused quite crossly. 'Does your poor toothy hurt?' inquired Pig-wig. Pigling Bland grunted.

Pig-wig ate the peppermint herself and followed the opposite side of the road. 'Pig-wig! keep under the wall, there's a man ploughing.' Pig-wig crossed over, they hurried down hill towards the county boundary.

Suddenly Pigling stopped; he heard wheels.

Slowly jogging up the road below them came a tradesman's cart. The reins flapped on the horse's back, the grocer was reading a newspaper.

'Take that peppermint out of your mouth, Pig-wig, we may have to run. Don't say one word. Leave it to me. And in sight of the bridge!' said poor Pigling, nearly crying. He began to walk frightfully lame, holding Pig-wig's arm.

The grocer, intent upon his newspaper, might have passed them, if his horse had not shied and snorted. He pulled the cart cross-ways, and held down his whip. 'Hallo! Where are *you* going to?'—Pigling Bland stared at him va-cantly.

'Are you deaf? Are you going to market?' Pigling nodded slowly.

'I thought as much. It was yesterday. Show me your licence?'

76

Pigling stared at the off hind shoe of the grocer's horse which had picked up a stone.

The grocer flicked his whip—'Papers? Pig licence?' Pigling fumbled in all his pockets, and handed up the papers. The grocer read them, but still seemed dissatisfied. 'This here pig is a young lady; is her name Alexander?' Pig-wig opened her mouth and shut it again; Pigling coughed asthmatically.

The grocer ran his finger down the advertisement column of his newspaper—'Lost, stolen or strayed, 10s. reward.' He looked suspiciously at Pig-wig. Then he stood up in the trap, and whistled for the ploughman.

'You wait here while I drive on and speak to him,' said the grocer, gathering up the reins. He knew that pigs are slippery; but surely, such a *very* lame pig could never run!

'Not yet, Pig-wig, he will look back.' The grocer did so; he saw the two pigs stock-still in the middle of the road. Then he looked over at his horse's heels; it was lame also; the stone took some time to knock out, after he got to the ploughman.

'Now, Pig-wig. NOW!' said Pigling Bland.

Never did any pigs run as these pigs ran! They raced and squealed and pelted down the long white hill towards the bridge. Little fat Pig-wig's petticoats fluttered, and her feet went pitter, patter, pitter, as she bounded and jumped.

They ran, and they ran, and they ran down the hill, and across a short cut on level green turf at the bottom, between pebble beds and rushes.

They came to the river, they came to the bridge—they crossed it hand in hand—then over the hills and far away she danced with Pigling Bland!